Some Other Books by Mary Stolz

BELLING THE TIGER

THE BULLY OF BARKHAM STREET

A DOG ON BARKHAM STREET

FRÉDOU

THE GREAT REBELLION

THE MYSTERY OF THE WOODS

THE NOONDAY FRIENDS

Maximilian's World

Maximilian's World

by
Mary Stolz

Pictures by Uri Shulevitz

HARPER & ROW, PUBLISHERS

New York

MAXIMILIAN'S WORLD

Text copyright © 1966 by Mary Stolz
Pictures copyright © 1966 by Uri Shulevitz

Printed in the United States of America. All rights reserved. No part of this book may be used or reproduced in any manner whatsoever without written permission except in the case of brief quotations embodied in critical articles and reviews. For information address Harper & Row, Publishers, Incorporated, 49 East 33rd Street, New York, N.Y. 10016.

Library of Congress Catalog Card Number: 66–12533

To Sharon Park

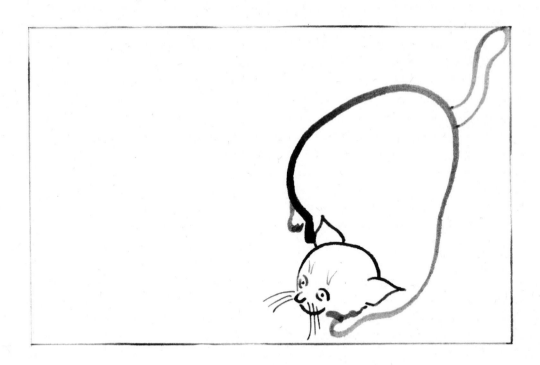

Siri, the big old delicatessen cat, was going from place to place, peering under chairs, behind doors, around corners. He was looking for something but couldn't remember what.

"Now, what could it be?" he asked himself as he prowled. *"What* could it be?"

Something to eat? But he wasn't hungry. Asa and Rambo, the mouse brothers? He had just left them half an hour before. His ping-pong ball? It was right over there under the sofa.

"Now, let me think," said the cat. He sat down to wash his paws as Maximilian, the little dog, came prancing down the hall from the delicatessen.

"Ah, there you are," said Siri happily. "I've been looking for you." He realized now that of course it was Maximilian he'd been seeking.

"What for?" said the little dog.

"I want to recite a poem to you. I just recited it to the mice. They were thrilled."

"Oh," said Maximilian.

"Poets," said Siri, "have always been partial to cats, demonstrating not only the beauty of their natures but also their good sense."

"How?" said Maximilian.

"Take, for instance," Siri went on, "the great poet, Dr. Samuel Johnson. You have, of course, heard of Dr. Johnson?"

Poets, said Siri,
have always been
partial to cats

"No," said Maximilian. "I've heard of Pancho Villa."

"Dr. Johnson lived with a cat named Hodge. There is a poem about them which I just happen to know by heart. Now, let's see . . . ah, yes . . ."

He began the recital.

For a verse or two Maximilian tried to concentrate. But presently that thing happened which always happened when Siri recited poetry or told stirring tales of his past. Maximilian got restless. Big yawns rocked his head. An itchy sensation made his fur bristle and his nose quiver.

He started to dance about lightly on his tiny feet, his clattery nails skipping on the floorboards. Siri broke off with a frown.

"Max," he said. "You are giving me less than your best attention."

"Yes," Maximilian admitted.

"Settle down."

"Yes, *amigo.*"

"I'm afraid you have no taste for the arts. However, I am confident that we can remedy this."

"I'm not."

"I believe I'll start a little school for you. Each day we will have a reading from one of the masters, and then a history period. I will tell you my history. This will be followed by a question and answer period. Now, we shall consider the poetry class over for today and go on to the next class. History. Did I ever tell you how I happened to leave my last home and take up this position as Cat to Benn's Delicatessen?"

"Yes."

"It's an uplifting tale, rather on the order of the Icelandic stories of heroism and hardihood. You might take notes, Maxie."

"I can't write."

"In your head." Siri couldn't write either. "One can keep an impressive store of facts in the head."

Maximilian wasn't going to argue that, as he was sure they would never get to the end of Siri's store of facts.

"My tale," said the cat, "begins in a house in this town, where I and the mice Asa and Rambo conducted our friendship under trying circumstances. They were being bullied and abused by a Head Mouse named Portman. He cut a large figure in the mouse world and didn't know there was any other. And *I* was constantly being threatened by the people of the house. They proposed to bring in a dog! As if I'd put up with such a thing."

Maximilian gasped, and Siri looked at him with surprise. "Oh, my goodness," he said. "How thoughtless of me. I do beg your pardon, Max. The fact is, I keep forgetting you *are* a dog," he said in a complimentary fashion. "I look upon you as my son."

Maximilian, who looked upon Siri as his father but still thought of himself as a dog, was so confused that he didn't know what to think. He decided to work it out later. After he'd eaten perhaps.

"So I left that house," Siri continued, "and headed for the wide world on my wild lone."

"You didn't get very far."

"Well, that's another story, and distance is not always a matter of miles. After a time I took up residence in this excellent delicatessen, where the people attend to my comfort in a manner proper to a cat. And they are not always threatening me with *dogs*."

He's forgotten again, thought Maximilian mournfully, trying to stay settled down and attentive. But Siri went on and on, and presently Maximilian began to itch and yawn and skip about.

"Why are you jumping around that way?" Siri demanded.

"Oh, no reason, *amigo*. Just—you know—jumping." Maximilian jumped a bit more to show how that was all he was doing.

"Siri," he said, "couldn't we go and see Asa and Rambo?"

I'm comfortable

"Not right now. I'm comfortable."

Siri couldn't explain it, but recently, every time the mouse brothers were mentioned or even when he thought of them, he got this sort of sad feeling. He'd had it a little while ago, even when reciting to them.

To test this, he said, "Speaking of Asa and Rambo, have you heard how they ran away from

Portman's tyranny and came to settle down here under my protection?" Yes, distinctly, as he spoke, he felt a wave of sorrow.

Why should that be?

Maximilian hadn't heard the story from the mice but had had several versions from Siri.

"I can't understand," Asa had said once to Maximilian, "why Siri's stories bore you. He never tells one twice in the same way."

"But I don't want to hear it even the first way," Maximilian had wailed. "I don't like so much talking. I want to play."

"Well, you're just a puppy," Asa had said kindly. "I suppose you can't help being restless."

"Well, you're just a mousie," Maximilian had pointed out.

"Yes," Asa had agreed. "But you see," he explained, "you have had such a sheltered life.

Rambo and I have had many adventures. Adventures are aging."

Maximilian, it was true, had never had an adventure. He wasn't confident that he would know how to have one if he got the chance. But he was very sure he wanted one.

"Siri, *amigo,*" he said now, "let us have an adventure."

Siri sighed. "I was just telling you about one."

"Is that the same as having one?"

"No," said Siri, and sighed again. "No, not quite."

He sounded so unhappy that Maximilian stopped talking about adventures.

"Siri," he said, "let's play. Let's run around and knock something over, so Mr. Benn will come and tell us to stop acting like cats and dogs. Let's make a noise. You miaow, and I'll yip."

He lifted his small head and let out a ribbon of *yip, yip, yip, yip*'s. . . .

"Oh, for goodness' sake," said Siri, closing his eyes. "Go and find the mice. Play with them." There it was again, that sorrowful, sorrowful feeling. He put his paws over his eyes.

Maximilian had got the mice so they would come out of their hole and play with him. He dearly loved a game of tag in the dim and spicy storeroom among the bins and bottles.

Asa and Rambo, though they admired Siri deeply, never for a moment forgot that he was a cat. In all the time they had known him, it had always been from the other side of a mousehole. As Rambo pointed out to his brother, friendship is as friendship does, but a mouse must keep first things first.

He and Asa had conducted this friendship

using a wall and a mousehole to make clear *first* that Siri was a cat and they were mice, and *second* that they were all good friends.

On the other hand they were always forgetting that Maximilian was a dog. It was Maximilian's opinion that most of the time they took him for another mouse.

"Caramba!" he would say to himself. He, practically a grandee, a Chihuahua undoubtedly descended from the Aztecs, to be taken here for a cat, there for a mouse! What would his ancestors say?

Still, he would think as he searched for his democratic friends, still, one could not complain. He had a wonderful father in the cat, and two fine playfellows in the mice. Ancestors were very well but, being dead and gone, made poor companions.

Now as Maximilian skipped off on his clattery

little toes Siri curled up with his head on all four paws and put his tail across his nose.

"All that dog wants to do is play," he grumbled to himself. How much there was to forgive in a puppy! Especially, he thought, growing tender-hearted, especially a puppy whose only father is a cat, which generally speaking might puzzle any dog.

And now he was gone to the mice again. Well that was right, perfectly all right. . . . Trying to go to sleep, Siri kept telling himself that he didn't mind a bit. There was not, as he frequently told Asa and Rambo, a jealous bone in his body. Not one.

Finally he did manage to get to sleep and had a dream in which he was back in that other house and was somehow a dog himself, confronted by Asa and Rambo, who had become cats wearing

Finally he
did manage
to get to
sleep and
had a dream

sombreros. He twitched and mewed and the tip of his tail flicked furiously.

Meanwhile, Maximilian had danced off to the storeroom, where he went directly to the mouse-hole in the wainscoting and called out, "Asa and Rambo, are you there, *amigos?*"

The mice came to their entrance, paused to be sure that Maximilian was alone, and came out.

"*Buenos días,*" said Rambo. "*Cómo esta?*"

"*Muy bien, gracias. Y ustedes?*" replied Maximilian.

"*Muy bien,*" said Asa. "*Gracias,*" he added quickly.

Maximilian was trying to teach the mice Spanish but didn't believe in too much classwork. Now, the greetings over, he said, "I've come to play."

At the word *play,* the three young animals began to skip around among boxes and barrels and

bottles and bales, among products from Italy and Scandinavia, from Portugal and Alaska, from all the seas and lands and deserts of the world.

When they had played for a long time, Maximilian flopped panting on the floor and gazed out the window. It was a beautiful day, and the backyard garden looked like the whole world to Maximilian.

He had been born in a kennel, transported from it to the delicatessen, and except for a walk in the garden with Siri on the very first night of his arrival, had never got out again. Mr. and Mrs. Benn felt he was too young for the risks involved.

He stared and stared at the world. There was a lilac tree in it and rows of potting shelves. There was a hive of honey bees. And over it all was a wonderful blue sky with clouds like piles of pot cheese.

"Oh, do let's go out there, *amigos,*" he pleaded. "Let us go out and have an adventure."

"Certainly not," said Rambo just as Asa said, "Well, I'm not sure, Maxie—"

"What do you mean, you're not sure?" Rambo demanded of his brother. "You know quite well that when we settled down to be storeroom mice at Siri's invitation, we agreed we'd *never* go outside again."

Asa said nothing, so Rambo turned to Maximilian. "You see," he explained, "we had some terrible experiences out there when we were getting from our old house to this one. Terrible," he repeated.

"But Siri says you were world travelers," Maximilian protested. As the mice almost never talked about their past, contrary Maximilian was always trying to get stories out of them. "He says you sailed on a ship to a faraway land and defied a dictator and had *adventures*. All sorts of adventures."

At his words Asa's face took on a dreaming expression. He was thinking of a jungle and a tiger with a blue-belled collar on its tail, a collar put there personally, with their own paws, by him and Rambo.

"Ah, yes," he murmured. "Adventure."

But Rambo's mind had gone immediately to the fearful trip he and Asa had taken when they ran away from Portman, the high-handed Head Mouse of the only other house they had ever known. What a journey it had been! He recalled the night and the rain, the fierce creatures of the field, the loneliness and fright. He remembered how in desperation they had fled into this storeroom, where Siri had given them haven.

He and his brother were Siri's debtors. They were also his audience, his admirers, his friends. They had promised never to leave him, and they had promised each other never to leave the store-room.

They had had enough adventure to last a mouse's lifetime.

So when Asa began, "Ah, yes—" Rambo scowled and said, "Asa, don't give him false hopes."

"I don't know about false, Rambo. I mean, we could just whisk out there and back, couldn't we? Through that little hole in the screen. After all, poor little Maxie should have an adventure."

"Poor little Maxie can whisk out there and have an adventure by himself. We'll watch and applaud from the windowsill."

Maximilian looked alarmed. He didn't think

he wanted to have an adventure all by himself. "I expect it would be more fun to share—" he began.

"Suppose," Rambo went on, ignoring him, "just suppose that after we three had whisked out, Mr. Benn found the hole in the screen and fixed it? What then? He'd let Max back in, of course, but how about us? Suppose a *real* cat found us before there was time to whisk back? Suppose—"

"Oh, Rambo," said Asa. "You used to be so stouthearted."

"When there was no choice. When we couldn't help it. We sailed to the faraway land because we couldn't get off the ship, and we ran away from Portman because it is intolerable to live under a dictatorship."

"Here you live under the floorboards," said Maximilian. "What's the difference?"

The two mice stared at him in surprise. "You

mean you don't know what a dictatorship is?" said Rambo.

"No," said Maximilian. Siri had described dictatorships to him many times, but as Maximilian had scarcely listened to a word, he had learned nothing. "Is it like an umbrella?" he guessed. He had seen Mr. and Mrs. Benn's umbrella and knew

it was something they got under. "A bed?" Siri was fond of sleeping under beds, but perhaps mice didn't like them. "A cloud? A packing crate?"

"My goodness," said Asa. "What ignorance!"

Maximilian looked uncomfortable. He decided it was a good thing Siri was going to start a school for him. He decided he was going to listen carefully in class and take notes in his head. He, a member of the Mexican nobility, to be called ignorant by a mouse!

Rambo was explaining how in some parts of the world mice lived under the iron claws of despots like Portman, who allowed them no rights, no freedom, no choice in how their own lives were to go.

Maximilian's eyes grew bigger and bigger. "Why don't *all* the mice run away from him?" he asked at last.

Rambo looked sad. "I suppose they don't know they can. Or they're scared."

"They should have a revolution," said Maximilian, his Mexican blood stirring. He wasn't exactly sure what a revolution was either, but any right-thinking Mexican has the word on the tip of his tongue. "A revolution, that's the answer." The more he said it, the surer he was of the meaning.

"Maybe they will, one day," said Rambo. "A mouse can be put upon just so long, you know."

"You two weren't put upon long," said Maximilian respectfully.

Asa preened himself a bit, but Rambo looked anxious. He knew how Asa's mind was working. A world traveler, a revolutionary, to be afraid of whisking out to the backyard? To be cowardly in the sight of an idealistic young puppy? *Unthinkable,* Asa would be thinking. *Unthinkable!*

"Asa," said Rambo sternly. "I *forbid* this venture. I will not *permit* you to whisk out there."

Maximilian blinked. Never had he heard such a tone in Rambo's voice before. Or in anyone's voice. Asa, staring at his brother, seemed confounded. There was silence for a long while, and then Asa said a crushing thing.

"Rambo," he said, "you sound just like Portman."

And he headed for the hole in the screen with Maximilian skipping after him, to the wild backyard.

Rambo crept miserably through the hole in the wainscoting to their tunnel under the floorboards. It was the first time he had ever been in there alone, and he huddled in a corner, angry and then unhappy. Angry, unhappy.

After the first moment of alarm and the first
dazzle of the sun, Asa and Maximilian began to
dash about the yard, squeaking and yipping. Then
they climbed up to the potting shelf to look at the
world from above. Asa had no trouble mounting a
pile of boxes, but Maximilian, who was not much
bigger than the mouse, had a fearful time; and
when he finally did reach the shelf, all the boxes
tipped over and spilled across the ground.

"Now what will I do?" he asked Asa.

They peered over the edge.

"Let's think about it later," Asa suggested.
"Let's just rest here for a minute."

Maximilian was always happy to think about
something later, so they stretched out at full length
on the shelf, and the sun spilled over them like hot
silk.

"Isn't the world splendid, *amigo?*" said Maximilian after a while. He gave a yip of joy.

Asa was too kind to point out that this was not the world but only the backyard and garden of a delicatessen. After all, it was part of the world, and small animals couldn't take it all in at once.

So he agreed and closed his eyes. He seemed to hear more than when they were open. There was a lovely fiddling sound, for instance, that he hadn't noticed before. What could it be?

"Look, Asa," said Maximilian, prodding him. "Look at those tiny green creatures down there. Who are they?"

Asa looked. "They're grasshoppers."

"They make music."

"So they do."

The two small adventurers stared at the musicians.

"Maximilian," Asa said excitedly. "Do you know they're making that music with their hind legs? They're just rubbing them together. See?"

"Let's try that," said Maximilian.

Asa rubbed his hind legs together as fast as he could, but no sound came at all. He decided he wasn't musical, and stopped, but Maximilian tried so hard that he fell off the potting shelf.

Asa ran down a rake handle and over to the dog, who was shaking the dust off his coat. "Are you hurt, Maxie?" he asked anxiously.

"Not at all," said Maximilian cheerfully. "Anyway," he added, "it's one way of getting down."

They laughed and then got into conversation with the grasshoppers, who admitted they didn't know how they made music with their hind legs.

"Some can and some can't," said the greenest grasshopper, who was the concertmaster.

Some
can and,
some can't

Asa and Maximilian agreed that that was about it. Presently the sun sank behind the fence. The yard grew shadowy.

"I think we'd better go in," said Asa.

"Will we come out into the world again?" Maximilian pleaded.

"Of course," said Asa, hoping he could get Rambo to come next time.

But Rambo, when his brother came chattering gaily into the tunnel, turned his back.

"Rambo," said Asa. "Don't be angry. Really, you should go out there too." He told about the grasshoppers and the sunlight and Maximilian's way of getting off the potting shelf. "Oh, you ought to come with us, Rambo. Truly, you ought."

From Rambo, silence and an immovable, reproachful back.

Asa talked on with less enthusiasm. At length his voice died away altogether, and there was no sound in the tunnel for a long time.

Then Asa spoke again. "All right, Rambo," he said. "All right. If this is how you want to be, all right. I won't talk to you too."

Whereupon he turned his back on Rambo's back and stopped talking.

And so it went.

Every day Asa and Maximilian flicked their tails and darted through the screen, leaving Rambo and Siri disconsolate and cross behind them.

And every day when the two backyard adventurers returned, Maximilian found Siri sleeping on top of something, where he couldn't be reached, and Asa found Rambo's back turned to him.

"Siri, *amigo*," Maximilian would call up to the cat on the bureau or the table or the bookcase, "Siri, when does school open? I have discovered in me a great thirst for learning."

But Siri would sleep, or seem to sleep. And the

mouse brothers continued silent, facing away from each other.

It was sad.

Everyone in the delicatessen was upset. Except, of course, Mr. and Mrs. Benn. They didn't know Siri and Maximilian were out of sorts, and they didn't know Asa and Rambo were there. The Benns kept their large cat and their small dog, assuming that between them the mouse matter was under control. By under control Mr. and Mrs. Benn meant no mice, which showed they certainly didn't know their cat and dog well.

One day Rambo was sitting on the storeroom windowsill, staring at the adventurers in the sunny backyard.

Maximilian had taken off his sombrero and was doing a Mexican hat dance around it. There were a

whole lot of grasshoppers, who had nothing better to do, fiddling him a tune. Bees leaned out of the lilacs to look.

Asa, who'd been sitting very still on the potting shelf, spied Rambo at the window. He leaped down to jig along after Maximilian, looking as south-of-the-border as a New England seaport mouse could well manage.

"They look very *très gai,* don't they?" said a soft sudden voice at Rambo's side.

Rambo looked up in horror, decided his end had come, and wondered if he really cared. Here he was, right next to Siri, *with no wall in between.*

"Good-bye, Asa," he said in his heart. "I'm sorry we ended it all in silence, and I hope you will always understand that I spoke under stress and for your own good. . . ."

As he'd expected to be swallowed before this

speech was over, he slid a glance sideways to see what was holding Siri up.

The big cat wasn't even looking at him. He was regarding with melancholy eyes the revelry in the backyard. He seemed not even to be aware that the figure at his side was a mouse.

Rambo realized that to Siri he was just a fellow sufferer. Oh, my, he thought. Poor Siri. So proud and self-confident, to be brought low by a bit of a dog.

"I found a jealous bone in my body too," he offered in an attempt to share the cat's humiliation.

"So that's what it is," said Siri glumly. "I was beginning to think so. Nothing dignified, nothing profound, like sorrow. Only common jealousy. A base emotion."

He transferred his gaze from Rambo to the yard again and lapsed into brooding. "Dancing dogs,"

he muttered after a few moments. "I brought that pup up from a puppy. I tended him, protected him, instructed him, entertained him, enlightened him. What didn't I do for that Chihuahua?"

"You didn't let him alone," Rambo said abruptly, surprising himself as much as Siri. "I didn't let Asa alone either, and that's a fact."

Siri, for once, had nothing to say. He shifted his gaze from the backyard again and fixed steady eyes on the mouse at his side.

Rambo hunched a little but resisted the urge to flee. After all, Siri had been his and Asa's friend and protector too. He had entertained and instructed and enlightened them. He had given them a home. Now Siri was in need of comfort and counsel, and Rambo determined to offer what he could, no matter that his instinct was instructing him to run away.

There is a time to run, and a time to remain, thought Rambo, who hadn't listened to Siri quoting literature all this time for nothing. This was a time to remain.

"Asa said I was just like Portman," he began.

"Oh, villainous!" cried Siri. "What ingratitude is here!"

"Siri!" Rambo shouted. "Let me continue."

Siri subsided, muttering, "Knaves, ingrates—"

"Now, now," Rambo said soothingly. "Now, now. You see," he went on, "our trouble is that we're overprotective. Maybe, in a different way, I am like Portman. Maybe you are too."

"Watch whom you're calling a dictator," growled Siri. "To say nothing of a mouse."

Rambo debated whether to be insulted by the last observation, then decided against it, since Siri was under great tension.

"Portman," Rambo continued firmly, "told us mice what we should do for *his* own good. You and I tell Max and Asa what to do for *their* own good. Maybe it isn't too much better that way."

Siri moved his tail around and regarded the tip of it twitching slowly. Rambo regarded it too but nervously stood his ground.

"You know, Rambo," Siri said at long length, "you are a wise and perceptive mouse. A mouse among mice, if I may put it that way."

"Oh, please do," said Rambo, who didn't see how Siri could have put it better. "Do, by all means."

"A mouse among mice," Siri repeated obligingly. "What you have just said has opened my eyes. You have put a fresh perspective on the situation."

He was looking more alert, and Rambo began

to feel that the time to remain was running out and the time to run was fast approaching.

"Look, Siri!" he cried out. "I believe they're coming back."

Siri looked and Rambo ran.

Once he was under the floorboards in the tunnel behind the wainscoting, Rambo called out, "Excuse me for talking and running, Siri. I just remembered something that couldn't wait."

"A wise and perceptive mouse," said Siri again, and tactfully left the storeroom so that the returning Asa might cross at his leisure and not in an undignified scuttle.

Siri valued dignity for others as well as for himself.

Meanwhile, out in the garden, Maximilian had wandered away from Asa, who was trying to explain to the grasshoppers just what a tiger consisted of.

"Miles and miles of black-and-yellow stripes," he was saying, "and wild gold eyes, and one swish of his tail would wreck our whole garden." He swept a paw and the grasshoppers jumped. "Wreck it," Asa repeated with satisfaction.

Maximilian, who wasn't yet actually tired of tiger tales, felt he wanted something different just

now. He didn't know what he wanted or where it was to be found. Like Siri before him, he wandered restlessly, looking here, poking his nose there.

Suddenly, behind a lilac bush, a shadow stirred. Maximilian moved forward cautiously, then made a little rush of delight. Of course! That was what he wanted! That was Siri there in the lilacs, waiting for him.

He pranced into the thicket, came out yelping, his popping eyes aghast.

"Tiger!" he yelled. "Tiger in the lilacs, Asa! *Vamos, vamos! Pronto, pronto, pronto!*"

Asa cast one quick glance toward the lilac bush, saw a shadowy figure that, even if only Siri-sized, bore a horrifying resemblance to the tiger of his past and of his dreams.

He and Maximilian almost got wedged in the

hole on their way back to the storeroom, and they parted without a word, each being anxious to reach comfort and safety.

But once through the mousehole, Asa disconsolately turned his back on Rambo. His head drooped forward until his tiny black nose rested on the floorboards.

"Asa?" said Rambo.

Asa spun around. "Yes, Rambo?"

"I wish to apologize."

"Oh, no," said Asa. "No, no, not at all, Rambo. It is I who should apologize for my recklessness."

"No, Asa. I was overbearing."

"And I was foolhardy."

"I have learned something in the past few days," Rambo persisted. "I have learned that love doesn't give anyone the right to dominate a fellow creature, any more than power gives him the right."

"I've learned something too," said Asa.

"What is that, Asa?"

"That there's a cat in the lilacs out there."

Rambo shuddered.

"Not a cat like Siri either," Asa added.

"There is no other cat like Siri," Rambo declared.

"So," Asa went on, "I believe that I'll play with you and Max in the storeroom from now on. Siri can go out with him and lie on the potting shelf. And Max can play with the grasshoppers. *They'll* keep him jumping."

Rambo sighed with relief but was wise enough not to comment further. "Where is Maxie?" he said instead.

"He went to find Siri. Maximilian can be without Siri only for a short time, you know. Then he gets lonely for him. Maxie needs Siri. So I do hope

Siri will come off the table and be a father again."

Maximilian finally found Siri asleep beneath the sofa in the Benns' living room.

"*Amigo?*" he whispered, joyous at finding Siri on the floor once again. "Siri, *amigo*. Let me tell you of my adventures."

"*Adventures!*" Siri began to scoff, but he opened his eyes and met the bright popping gaze of his little charge. His heart quite melted.

"Adventures, eh?" he said. "Well, well. Tell me all about it."

Adventure, after all, was where you found it. If the little dog thought it was to be found in their own backyard, if he considered that there he had the world, why, so much the better.

"Tell away, Maximilian," said the big cat.

"Well, to begin with," said Maximilian, "there's a tiger out there in the lilac bushes."

Well, to begin with,
said Maximilian

"Tiger?" said Siri, quirking a whisker.

"Indeed, a tiger," said Maximilian, panting with excitement. "Miles and miles of black-and-yellow stripes and wild gold eyes and—"

"In the lilac bushes you say?"

"Yes, and one swish of his tail—"

"He's a lazy old tom who wouldn't lift a paw to get a lobster dinner."

"*Oh?*" said Maximilian. "Oh. Are you sure?"

"Quite sure," said Siri smoothly, but then at Maximilian's downcast air was ashamed of himself. "He was a fierce fellow in his day though. No doubt some of that air still clings to him."

Maximilian brightened. "That must have been it. He has a tiger *air*."

"All right, all right," said Siri, slightly put out at this stir over another cat. "Go on with your ad-

ventures, Maxie. Tell away, tell away."

Maximilian told away. He went on and on and on. He mentioned each grasshopper by name, described every flower and bush, every tool and pot in the yard and garden. He gave great attention to detail. He provided an exhaustive and inaccurate history of the Mexican hat dance. He recounted each and every game he and Asa had devised and then explained at tremendous length how in all this he had missed his cat-father.

Gratified though he was to find he had been missed, Siri distinctly began to experience an odd sensation. Yawns shoved at his jaw, his whiskers stiffened, his nose quivered.

But indeed this was terrible! Was *this* what a long story did to the listener?

From now on, the cat vowed to himself, I shall seek the brevity of wit. Or do I mean the wit of brevity? I shall cut my stories short. A yawn he could not suppress overcame him.

"I entreat your pardon, Max," he said contritely. "It's just that I haven't been sleeping well lately."

"I understand," said Maximilian.

He was so happy to be back in his father's favor that he didn't care what Siri did, just so they could be together while he did it. Maximilian pondered over what he could do to show the cat how wonderful he was.

Of course! The perfect solution!

"*Amigo,*" he said. "*Por favor.* Tell me a story."

Siri yawned again. He looked down at the little

round head of his adopted puppy whose eyes gleamed like dark gems, whose ears flopped loosely like flower petals.

There was Maximilian, eagerly awaiting a story at last.

Now, if I weren't so drowsy, Siri said to himself, it would make me laugh.

Sleep, like a shadow, crept across his eyes.

"*Mañana*," he said softly. "I'll tell you a story when school opens. . . . *Mañana*," he repeated, and fell asleep.